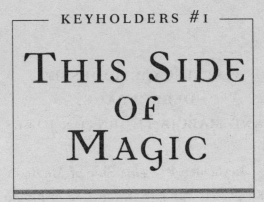

KEYHOLDERS #1

THIS SIDE
OF
MAGIC

D0038797

STARSCAPE BOOKS BY
DEBBIE DADEY
AND MARCIA THORNTON JONES

Keyholders #1: *This Side of Magic*

Keyholders #2: *The Other Side of Magic*

COMING SOON:

Keyholders #3: *Inside the Magic*

Keyholders #4: *The Wrong Side of Magic*

THIS SIDE OF MAGIC

Debbie Dadey and Marcia Thornton Jones

Illustrated by Adam Stower

A TOM DOHERTY ASSOCIATES BOOK • NEW YORK

This is a work of fiction. All of the characters, organizations, and events portrayed in this novel are either products of the author's imagination or are used fictitiously.

KEYHOLDERS #1: THIS SIDE OF MAGIC

Copyright © 2009 by Debra S. Dadey and Marcia Thornton Jones
The Other Side of Magic excerpt copyright © 2009 by Debra S. Dadey and Marcia Thornton Jones

Illustrations and map copyright © 2009 by Adam Stower

A Starscape Book
Published by Tom Doherty Associates, LLC
175 Fifth Avenue
New York, NY 10010

www.tor-forge.com

ISBN-13: 978-0-7653-5982-7
ISBN-10: 0-7653-5982-0

First Edition: May 2009

Printed in the United States of America

0 9 8 7 6 5 4 3 2 1

TO SUSAN COHEN—
for believing in book magic!—

AND KEVIN GABBARD—
*may the doors to peace, success, and happiness
always be opened to you*—MJ and DD

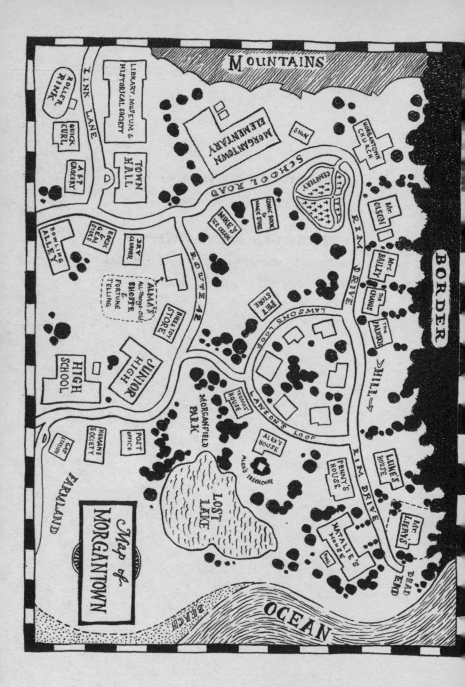

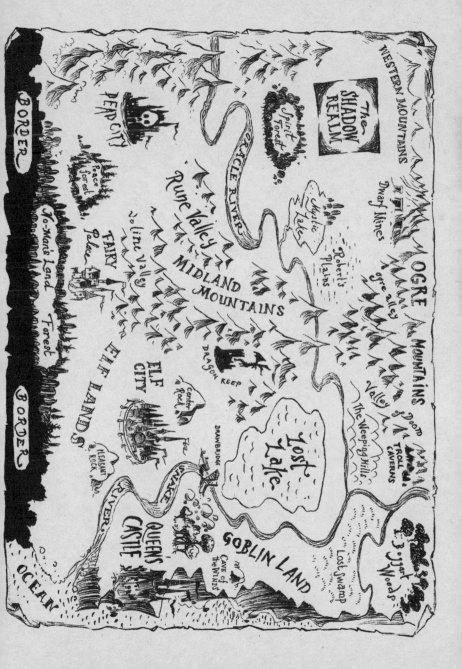

1

"Who's there?" Luke cried out. He clutched the basketball to his chest and jerked around. The hair stuck up on the back of his neck. He had the feeling that someone—or something—was watching him from the dark woods behind his house.

"What are you doing?" his best friend Penny asked. "Just shoot the ball."

Luke gave the woods one more nervous glance, shrugged, and tossed the ball in the basket. Swish!

Penny wasn't surprised. Luke hardly ever

missed. He was the best shooter on their fifth-grade team. She grabbed the ball for her turn.

"Sorry," Luke said. "I have this creepy feeling that something is watching me."

"That's so weird. I've felt the same way for the last couple of days," Penny said.

The two kids peered at the border of thick bushes behind all the houses on Luke's side of the street. The last street of Morgantown. Beyond the bushes were giant trees. They were so tall they were impossible to see over. Nobody knew what was on the other side of the trees. When Penny was little, she thought the woods were the end of the world because the trees, vines, and bushes were so thick you couldn't see more than a few inches into them.

Luke couldn't remember anyone ever telling him not to go there, but for some reason he knew it was forbidden. Everybody did.

Snap! Crack! Thud!

"Did you hear that?" Luke asked Penny.

She nodded, her eyes wide. "There's something in there," she whispered.

Luke stepped toward the bushes. Penny dropped the ball and grabbed Luke's arm. "Don't get near those bushes. They're full of thorns. Besides, that's probably some wild animal we heard."

"Do you think it could be a wildcat?" Luke asked. He liked the idea that a wildcat might be so close. He pulled away from Penny and crept to the edge of the bushes.

"There are no wildcats in Morgantown," Penny said. "But there are snakes. Get back here and finish this game before a snake bites you."

But Luke didn't go back, he reached out and . . .

"Ouch!" he screamed.

Penny ran to him, ready to fight off a wild animal. "Did something bite you?"

Luke nodded. His face turned red. "Yes, one of these thorns jumped up and bit me." He looked at the small puncture mark on this thumb and at the thick blood-red thorns on the dark bush.

Penny rolled her eyes. "Sure it did."

"I'm serious, I think this bush did it on purpose."

Penny started to argue, but another noise made her stop. The sound came from behind Mr. Leery's house. Mr. Leery was Luke's next-door neighbor. "Whatever was back there is in those bushes now."

The bushes between Luke's neighbor's house and his house shook and a sleek, black animal slithered out.

"It's only Mo," Penny said. She picked up the neighbor's cat and scratched the tuft of hair that stood out between his ears. "Mo, you scared us to death."

"Mrrrr-roooookkk," Mo purred.

"What was he doing in the bushes?" Luke asked.

Penny plucked a bright orange feather from

his whiskers. "He was doing a little hunting," she said. "Come on, Mo. Let's get you home."

Mo placed his huge paws on Penny's shoulder. He peered back at the tangle of bushes as Penny carried him home.

Mo had lived next door to Luke with Mr. Leery for as long as the kids could remember. He wasn't the best-looking cat to roam the neighborhood. In fact, his huge paws, spotted chest, and the silly Mohawk of hair jutting up between his curling ears made him one of the ugliest cats they'd ever seen, but the kids would never tell Mr. Leery that. The only attractive thing about Mo was his silver collar decorated with a round purple stone, an amethyst.

Mr. Leery loved his cat. He even talked to Mo as if they were best friends.

Luke followed Penny over to Mr. Leery's old house. She pushed through the vines that hung on the porch of the small cottage to knock on the front door. "You know," Penny told Luke,

"Mr. Leery really needs to paint his house. This place is a mess."

The peeling paint and overgrown vines were only part of the problem with Mr. Leery's house. The fence in front of his home creaked in the breeze, it was so old. Gray, stringy moss hung from the giant tree branches in his overgrown yard. Some of the kids at school teased Luke about living next door to a haunted house, that's how bad it needed fixing up.

Luke shrugged. "Maybe he can't afford it."

"Then we should get some kids together and do it for his birthday," Penny suggested.

Penny and Luke had known Mr. Leery all their lives. He was like a grandfather to them. He even gave them presents on birthdays and holidays.

"When is his birthday anyway?" Luke asked.

This time Penny shrugged. She was surprised that she didn't know that about Mr. Leery. "I'll ask him if he ever opens the door."

She knocked again and Mr. Leery opened the door, but he was so upset that Penny forgot to ask him about his birthday. "Oh dear, oh dear," he said, wringing his large hands. "I'm glad you're here."

"What's wrong?" Luke asked.

"No, oh no. I definitely wasn't ready for this." Mr. Leery paced back and forth in the doorway. His bald head shone with sweat and his big nose was red with worry. Deep wrinkles lined his forehead.

Penny led him to a porch chair. "Just calm down and tell us what's wrong. Maybe we can help."

Mr. Leery sat down and took a deep breath. "Of course, you are right. I do need your help."

Penny nodded. "We'll do whatever we can."

Mr. Leery looked into Penny's dark brown eyes and Luke's clear green ones. "I have just received word that an associate of mine has died. I must leave for a few days."

"We're sorry about your associate," Penny said, remembering her grandfather. "It's so sad when someone dies."

"Thank you," Mr. Leery said. He rubbed his forehead before asking, "Could you possibly take care of Mo for me while I'm gone?"

Mo leaped out of Penny's arms and growled.

"Now Mo, no need to get testy with me," Mr. Leery told him. "Remember what I said. I need you to stay here and watch for . . . leaks."

Mo turned his back to Mr. Leery and licked a paw. Penny laughed. "Your cat acts like he understands every word you say."

"We'll be happy to feed Mo," Luke told Mr. Leery.

Mr. Leery nodded. "He is quite self-sufficient. But if you could stop by to . . . er . . . pet him every day I would appreciate it. And please, make sure he doesn't go out at night."

Mo hissed when Mr. Leery said the word *pet*.

"Sure," Penny said.

"I have these for you." Mr. Leery pulled two silver bracelets from the big pockets of his old blue robe. They each had a silver charm in the shape of a key on them.

"You don't have to give us anything," Luke said. The idea of wearing a silver bracelet was embarrassing. What would the guys on his basketball team say?

"Oh, but I do," Mr. Leery said seriously. "I want you to promise me that you'll wear these every day until I get back. They are protection."

"Protection from what?" Luke asked.

"Oh, just protection," Mr. Leery said mysteriously. "And a key to my house is on each one."

"Thanks," Penny said. "I'll be happy to wear it."

Luke sighed and held out his wrist.

Mr. Leery slipped the bracelets onto their wrists. Penny looked closely at hers. "Wow, this looks really old." The silver band was dented like someone had taken a hammer to it. Squiggly lines, circles, and strange shapes were engraved on the top. Embedded in the metal was a small green stone.

"They are very old. Please take very good care of them. Now, be on your way while I prepare for my trip," Mr. Leery said.

Luke and Penny walked down the sidewalk in front of Mr. Leery's house. A loud bang caused them to turn around. Mr. Leery was nailing an old horseshoe on his door.

Penny shook her head and whispered to Luke, "What's up with him? I've never seen him act so weird."

"His friend just died. Of course, he's going to be upset. Come on," Luke suggested. "Let's go finish our game." There was nothing Luke would rather do on a Friday afternoon than play basketball.

"What were you guys doing over at that old geezer's house?"

Luke groaned. Natalie, the nosiest girl in their class, stood on the sidewalk in front of them. In her right hand she carried a bright pink notebook. "I've been watching Mr. Leery," Natalie told them. "I know he's up to something."

Penny put her hands on her hips. "For your information, Mr. Leery is not an old geezer. He happens to be a very nice man and we're going to take care of his cat while he's away. He even gave us these bracelets to pay us."

Penny held up her bracelet before she realized her mistake. Natalie grabbed Penny's wrist and said, "Let me see that."

Penny pulled her arm away. "Get your own, this is mine."

Natalie stormed back to her big house across the street. "Fine, my daddy will buy one for me," she said over her shoulder. "He says that old Leery place is a firetrap anyway. He's probably going to have it condemned."

Luke looked at Penny. "Could her dad really do that?"

"Probably," Penny said. "Maybe we'd better be

nice to Natalie for a while. We don't want to get Mr. Leery in trouble."

Being nice to Natalie wouldn't be easy. Luke had never seen anyone more spoiled. She always got what she wanted.

"I think she's just jealous of us," Penny said.

"No way," Luke told her. "Natalie is the richest kid our age in Morgantown."

"Then why doesn't she just leave us alone?" Penny snapped.

Luke shrugged. "Too bad there are no other kids on this street for her to bug."

The next evening, Penny and Luke were out behind Luke's house playing basketball again. Penny was losing at the PIG game, so she was happy to hear a noise over at Mr. Leery's house.

"Listen," she told Luke. "Mr. Leery must have gotten back sooner than he expected."

"Let's go see him and give back these bracelets," Luke suggested. He really didn't want to wear a girly bracelet to school the next day.

Penny nodded. "Let's race!" Racing was something she could beat Luke at every time.

Penny made it to the porch first. She stopped short when she saw who was on the porch.

It definitely was not Mr. Leery.

2

A tall, thin boy stood on Mr. Leery's porch. He had knobby knees, buck teeth, and big ears. And he wore a pink tutu.

Luke couldn't help laughing out loud, but Penny tried to be nice. "Are you looking for Mr. Leery?"

"Yessssss," the boy said in a high-pitched voice. It sounded like a cartoon character. "Have you seen him?"

Luke snickered, but Penny poked him with her elbow. "Mr. Leery's out of town right now. He probably won't be back for a few days."

"A few days?" the kid squeaked.

"Yeah," Luke said. "Hey, why are you wearing that silly costume?"

"Costume?" the boy said, looking at Luke closely. "What do you mean?"

"Only girls wear stuff like that," Luke told him, pointing at the tutu.

"Not anymore," Penny told him. "Boys can wear whatever they want."

Luke shook his head. "Not at Morgantown Elementary. You'd get beat up if you wore something like that to school."

"That's not true," Penny said. "We have a very nice school."

"School?" the boy asked.

"Sure," Luke told him, pointing down the street. "It's just up that way. It's where kids go to be tortured."

"Very funny," Penny said. "We learn lots of important stuff there and you know it."

"Well, we do learn not to wear pink tutus," Luke said matter-of-factly.

The boy didn't act the least bit interested in school or pink tutus. "Has Leery had many visitors lately?" he asked.

"What's wrong with Mo?" Penny interrupted, pointing to Mr. Leery's front window. Mo was frantically scratching the glass, like he was dying to get out. When that didn't work he paced back and forth on the table by the window, spitting and swishing his tail.

"Look at his fur," Luke said. "It's sticking up so high, he looks like a panther."

The strange boy wasn't looking at Mo. He stared at three other boys standing beside Mr. Leery's front fence.

"Hey Luke, want to play some b-ball? My dad put up lights," Alex Dillon said. He twirled his basketball on the tip of his finger. He was the best dribbler on the Morgantown fifth-grade team, and he didn't hesitate to tell everyone.

"Maybe," Luke said. "I'll ask my mom."

A short kid named Thomas yelled, "Who's

your friend? Tinkerbell or the Tooth Fairy?" All three boys laughed like Thomas was some sort of comedian.

Penny put her hands on her hips. "Why don't you guys go pick your noses instead of picking on helpless kids?"

"Okeydokey," Alex said. "Let's go pick our noses." The three boys trotted off, pretending to pick their noses.

"Jerks," Penny muttered under her breath.

The boy with the tutu looked hard at Alex and his friends. "Do they know Leery?" he asked.

Luke nodded. "Sure, most people in town know Mr. Leery. Thomas delivers Mr. Leery's groceries every week. His dad owns the A&P. Alex is supposed to mow his yard."

The boy squeaked and ran down the steps. Actually, he didn't run. He tripped and fell flat on the sidewalk. Without a word he picked himself up and scrambled down the street.

"Wait a minute," Luke called after the kid.

"You didn't even tell us your name. We'll tell Mr. Leery you came by."

The boy didn't stop running. He went in the same direction as the boys, but before he got too close, Penny saw him duck behind some bushes.

"What a strange kid," Penny said.

"I hope he doesn't get beat up. He needs to get some normal clothes on," Luke said.

Penny shook her head. "He must be new to Morgantown. I've never seen him around here before."

"He sure asked a lot of questions," Luke said. "Maybe we shouldn't have told him anything about Mr. Leery."

"What could it hurt?" Penny asked.

"You're the one always saying we shouldn't talk to strangers."

"Yeah," Penny said. "But he's just a kid."

Mo let out a loud yowl that made the kids jump.

"Why doesn't he just come out through his pet door?" Penny asked, looking at Mo through the dusty window.

Luke released the hook that locked the small pet door at the bottom of the old wooden door. "That's weird. Someone locked Mo in. Why would anyone do that?"

Mo sprinted out the door as soon as Luke moved the rock, knocking Luke over. "Rowl!" Mo screeched and raced up and down the porch, looking all around the yard.

"Settle down, Mo," Penny said. "Mr. Leery will be back soon."

But Mo didn't settle down. He growled. He arched his back. He even hissed at the bushes lining the backyard. Penny and Luke looked, but they couldn't figure out what he was so mad about.

"Maybe I should take him home with me to-night," Penny suggested. "It'd be awful if he ran away before Mr. Leery got back."

"Are you sure your mom wouldn't mind?" Luke asked. Both kids had always wanted pets, but they'd never been able to talk their parents into anything other than goldfish.

Penny picked up Mo and petted him. "It'll just be for one night. Maybe Mom won't notice."

Luke shrugged. "Good luck with that."

"Come on, Mo," Penny said, snuggling Mo up to her neck. "Wouldn't you like to come home with me?"

To Penny's surprise, Mo roared and leaped out of her arms. He darted out onto the sidewalk and down the street.

"Wow," Luke said. "I've never seen him act like that before. I guess he really misses Mr. Leery."

"We have to find him," Penny cried as they followed Mo down the sidewalk. "It's getting dark and I still have that creepy feeling that someone is watching me."

Penny and Luke couldn't help glancing toward the woods. A chill ran down Luke's back. Sometimes he wished he didn't live so close to all that overgrown blackness.

Luke opened his mouth to tell Penny that someone should take a Weed Whacker to the woods, but he didn't get the chance. Just then, someone grabbed his shoulder. Hard.

3

"Ahhhhhh!" Luke screamed and twirled around, his hands in a karate-chop stance. Luke didn't actually know karate, but he thought if he looked like he knew something about breaking wood in half, his attacker would run away.

But, it wasn't an attacker. It was Natalie. And she didn't run. She rolled her eyes at Luke. "What is *your* problem?" she asked.

"*My* problem?" Luke sputtered, his hands still in front of his face ready to chop through the air. "*You're* the one sneaking up on people."

"I wasn't sneaking," Natalie explained. "You

just didn't hear me because that cat was making such a racket."

"Natalie's right," Penny said. "Mo was making so much noise we didn't hear her."

Luke glared at Penny. He couldn't believe Penny was taking Natalie's side. Natalie opened her pink notebook and wrote furiously. She didn't have an ordinary pencil. Hers was topped with an eight-armed, one-eyed rubber monster with bright pink hair. The arms of the ogre trembled in Natalie's grasp. "So you've heard him, too," she said.

That was just so Natalie. She would start talking as if everyone knew exactly what she was talking about. Luke knew that if he kept his mouth shut she would go away faster. But Penny couldn't help asking, "Heard who?"

"The cat," Natalie said.

Penny held up her arm to show where Mo's claws left four faint streaks of blood. "Of course, we heard Mo," she said. "Something about those boys irritated him."

Natalie tapped the ogre against her two front teeth. "You're wrong. As usual."

Now it was Penny's turn to think about karate-chopping Natalie, but Luke interrupted her before she could. "I know I'm going to be sorry for asking, but what in the world are you talking about?"

"You can't tell me you didn't hear it," Natalie said.

"Hear what?" Luke and Penny yelled at the same time.

Natalie bopped the ogre against the open pages of her notebook. "That cat talks. I've seen him chatting with Mr. Leery from my bedroom window."

"Did you actually hear him?" Penny asked.

"No," Natalie admitted, "it was too far away."

Penny shook her head. "Mr. Leery talks to Mo because he doesn't have anyone else to talk to. That's all it is."

"You're wrong," Natalie said, pointing her ogre pencil at Penny. "Mo answered Mr. Leery. I have it all documented in my notebook."

"Let me see," Luke said and lunged for Natalie's notebook, nabbing a corner. But Natalie hung on tight.

"Give. It. Back," Natalie said, accompanying each word with a jerk.

"No. Way," Luke said with two tugs of his own.

Penny had been itching to look at Natalie's spy book ever since Natalie started carrying it around in the middle of the summer. Now that school was well under way, Penny was sure Natalie had her pages filled with enough information to blackmail half of Morgantown, including Penny, Luke, and even Mr. Leery and Mo. Penny was just about to grab the notebook for herself when a movement caught the corner of her eye. She could've sworn it was a giant bird coming in for the kill.

"DUCK!" she screamed. Without thinking, she tackled Natalie around the ankles.

Natalie fell against Luke, sending the notebook sliding across the ground. All three tumbled in a heap just as a dark shadow swooped down upon them. Penny covered her head like a turtle. Luke rolled into a ball like an armadillo. Natalie scrambled after her notebook like a crab and looked toward the sky just as something big crash-landed into the bushes between Mr. Leery's house and Luke's.

"Did you see what it was?" Natalie asked. "I'm pretty sure it was a monster trying to grab us right off the face of the Earth." She opened her note-book and began furiously scribbling. "Wait until I tell my father. He'll call the police. He'll call the National Guard. He'll call the President!"

"And they'll all think you're one bowling pin short of a strike," Luke said as he dusted off his jeans. "Because there are no such things as flying monsters."

Natalie jabbed her pencil at Luke's nose, mak-ing the arms of the plastic ogre flop. "Then how do you explain what just crashed into those bushes?"

Before Penny and Luke could answer, the bushes rattled and rustled and wiggled. Some-thing was stuck in the thorns, and whatever it was,

it didn't sound happy. In fact, it almost sounded like it was muttering a string of words that Penny and Luke were never allowed to say or they'd end up being grounded until they were one hundred and two.

"W—wh—who's there?" Penny stammered.

She grabbed Luke's arm and pulled him back. Step-by-step, the three kids inched away from the shaking bushes. Natalie even forgot she was holding her notebook and it slipped to the ground. Suddenly, the leaves exploded from the bushes as a black shape broke free from the tangle of hedge with a cry of "RRRR-OUCH!"

"Mo!" Luke gasped at Mr. Leery's black cat. "You scared the snot out of us!"

Mo's fur was ruffled. Leaves were stuck in his whiskers and a bright red feather was caught in his tail. The cat looked at the three kids as if they were hairballs. He walked casually over to Natalie's notebook and slashed at the open pages with his giant paws.

"Stop that, you mangy cat," Natalie snapped.

Penny ignored Natalie and scooped up Mo. "Where have you been?"

"Mrrrrrr-arrrnd," Mo meowed.

"Did he just say 'around'?" Natalie asked.

"Of course not. He is a cat. Cats do not talk," Luke said slowly as if he were explaining things to a two-year-old.

"Maybe not most cats," Natalie said. "But I have a sneaking suspicion that Mo is not an ordinary cat and Mr. Leery is not an ordinary neighbor. It's all right here in my notebook."

"Don't be silly," Penny said as she plucked a thorn from between Mo's toes.

"Mrrrrr-ahhhnks," Mo said.

"See?" Natalie said. "He just said 'thanks.'"

"Oh, for crying out loud. He's just purring because he's glad to be safe," Luke said. "Don't you know anything about cats?"

"Maybe you're right," she said slowly. "I don't know enough yet. Give me the cat."

"What?" Penny gasped and clutched Mo a little tighter. Mo growled. She loosened her grip, but only a little.

"I need to find out if my suspicions are true," Natalie said. "Hand him over."

"I'm not giving you anything," Penny said, turning around to keep Mo out of Natalie's reach. "Mr. Leery told us to take care of his cat, and that's exactly what we're going to do."

Natalie clutched her notebook to her chest. She tapped the ogre against her chin and glared at Mo. "Fine, have it your way. For now. But I intend to get to the bottom of this. With or without your help."

With that, Natalie stomped down the sidewalk. Penny smoothed the fur on Mo's back and pulled his claws loose from her T-shirt. She tried to sneak Mo into her house, but Penny's mom met Penny and Luke at the front door. "Take that cat home right now," Mrs. Jones told them.

"But we're watching him for Mr. Leery," Penny told her mother.

Mrs. Jones was not convinced. "That cat will be much happier in his own home. Besides, he probably has fleas."

Five minutes later, Penny gently scooted Mo through the cat door Mr. Leery had built. As soon as the last of Mo's tail was safely inside, she hooked the door so he couldn't get out during the night.

"I wonder why Natalie is so curious about Mo," Luke said, looking at her big house across the street.

"I couldn't care less what Natalie does," Penny said, "as long as she keeps her grubby hands off Mo."

4

"Oh, no!" Penny yelped. "What happened?"

Luke and Penny stood outside Mr. Leery's house the next morning. It was Sunday. The two friends had shown up bright and early to feed Mo, but the hook to the cat door was loose and the flap swayed back and forth in the morning breeze.

"I hooked the cat door. I'm sure I did," Penny cried.

"You did," Luke said. "I saw it myself."

"Then how did it get unhooked?" Penny asked.

"Let's just hope Mo didn't decide to go roaming during the night," Luke said.

"Here kitty-kitty-kitty," Penny called.

Luke pounded on the door and yelled, "Hey, Mo. Where are you?"

"What are you doing?" Penny asked.

"Looking for Mo," Luke said.

Penny stared at Luke for a full ten seconds. "Mo is a cat. He is not going to answer the door just because you knocked on it."

"Oh, yeah," Luke said, and he stopped knocking on the door.

Penny shook the bracelet down to her wrist so she could slip the key Mr. Leery had given her into the lock. Slowly, the door creaked open.

Mr. Leery's cottage was the oldest house on the block. It was the smallest, too. Light struggled through the two tiny windows on either side of the door to show walls lined with bookshelves. Books were everywhere. Some books had at least an inch-thick layer of dust on them. Several old ones were piled on top of one another in a giant heap. Some were open and pages had been torn out. A small desk sat in a corner.

Penny sneezed. "Mr. Leery needs a house-keeper and a housepainter." Then she giggled at a thought. Luke's mom was always painting some-thing in his house. Right now, she was turning Luke's room into a basketball locker room. He even had a basketball hoop for his dirty clothes. "Your mom would love to get her hands on this place."

"Let's just find Mo," Luke said. "We can worry about redecorating later."

But Mo was nowhere to be seen.

"Here kitty-kitty-kitty," Penny called.

Nothing.

Two doors opened to other rooms. One door led to the kitchen where brightly colored bottles of herbs, spices, and oils cluttered the counter. It looked as if Mo hadn't touched any of his food from the day before, but two blue feathers lay near the back door.

"He must've caught his own dinner," Luke said.

The other door led to Mr. Leery's bedroom.

There was a cot, a small dresser, and a straight-backed chair. Tufts of cat hair were clumped in the middle of the bed, but Mo wasn't there.

One thing was perfectly clear. Mo was nowhere to be found.

"What are we going to do?" Penny flopped onto the cot, sending cat hair floating into the air. "We promised Mr. Leery we'd take care of Mo!"

"It's not our fault," Luke said. "We hooked the door. I know we did."

"Then who unhooked it?" Penny asked.

Penny and Luke looked at each other. "Natalie," they said at the exact same time.

Penny jumped up. "I'm going to give her a piece of my mind," she snapped as they hurried outside.

"Are you sure you have enough pieces to share?" Luke joked as he locked the door behind them.

"This is no laughing matter," Penny said. "Natalie catnapped Mo and now she's going to pay for it."

Penny and Luke marched across the street to the biggest house in all of Morgantown.

"Wait," Luke said. "You can't just go barging into Natalie's house this early in the morning. What will her father say?"

Natalie's father was a judge and Natalie always bragged about how her father put people in jail. Luke didn't really think it would happen, but he didn't like the idea of being sent to jail for interrupting Mr. Lawson's morning coffee.

"I don't care if the Lawsons are eating their Cheerios. And I don't care if Natalie's father is a judge. I am going to get Mo back, and I'm going to do it right now."

Penny leaned against the doorbell and didn't let up until she heard footsteps. The door flung open and there stood Natalie. As soon as Natalie saw who it was, she tried to slam the door. Luke jammed his sneaker in the door just in time.

"What are you doing here?" Natalie asked.

"We came to get Mr. Leery's cat," Penny said, pushing the door back open. "Let us in."

"Cat? What cat?" Natalie said.

Luke plucked a clump of cat hair off of Natalie's sweatshirt. He waved it in front of Natalie's nose. "The cat that belongs to this," he said.

Natalie sighed. "Fine. Come in. He's in my room."

Natalie led them up a curving staircase and stopped in front of a closed door at the end of a long hallway.

"I can't believe you stole Mr. Leery's cat," Luke said.

"I didn't steal him," Natalie said.

"Then what do *you* call it when you take something that doesn't belong to you?" Penny asked.

Natalie opened the door to her room. It looked like a bottle of stomach medicine had exploded. The walls were pink. The curtains were pink. The carpet was pink. Even the ceiling was pink.

"I, um, just thought Mo might be a little lonely," Natalie said. "I brought him here to, um, play. Don't worry. I treated Mo like a baby."

And that's exactly what Natalie had done. Mo

peered at the kids through the slats of a pink doll's cradle. A piece of cardboard from Natalie's science fair project was taped over the top, trapping the cat inside. Mo was wearing a baby dress and a frilly pink bonnet. He had been wrapped in a pink blanket with ruffles, but long claw marks were proof that he got loose from that in a hurry. His giant paws poked out from between the slats like a prisoner reaching through the bars of a cell.

When Luke snorted at the sight, Mo hissed.

"What have you done?" Penny asked, kneeling down to reach her fingers through the slats to scratch Mo under the chin.

"I told you, I treated him like a baby," Natalie said. "I wanted to see what he would say."

"Say?" Penny repeated. Then she noticed Natalie's notebook lying by the cradle. "You were teasing Mo just to see if he would talk?"

"Isn't that just the *cutest* thing you *ever* did see?"

All three kids jumped at the voice. There,

standing in the doorway, was Natalie's mother. Mrs. Lawson was almost as wide as she was tall. She wore her hair piled on top of her head, fuzzy slippers, and bright red lipstick. "Those are the very same baby clothes my sweet little Natalie wore when she was an itty-bitty baby herself. Doesn't that cat look just *precious?*"

Luke and Penny couldn't say Mo looked good dressed up like a baby. He looked ridiculous. But they didn't want to lie to an adult, so they both kept their mouths shut. It didn't matter.

"I *must* have a picture of this," Mrs. Lawson said as she gave Natalie a big hug. "It will look *adorable* in our photo album. Come along, dear, and I'll get you the camera."

Natalie grabbed her notebook and followed her mother out the door. "I'll be right back," she warned. "Don't touch a thing."

Natalie was barely out of sight when Mo growled. "BBbbbbout time."

"What did you say?" Penny asked Luke.

"I didn't say anything," Luke said. "I thought that was you."

Penny looked at Luke. Luke looked at Penny. Then they both looked at Mo.

Mo looked out the bars of the crib. "Gggrrrrr. . . . If you ask me," the cat muttered in a very human-sounding voice, "this is going above and beyond the call of duty."

"Holy moly," Luke gasped. "Natalie was right. You *can* talk!"

"RRRrrrr. . . . Of course I can talk," the cat muttered. "It's just that most people don't bother to lisssssten."

Penny plopped down on Natalie's bed. Luke steadied himself by holding on to the wall.

"But . . . but . . . but cats *can't* talk," Penny argued.

Mo blinked his amber eyes at her. "Okay," he said slowly. "If you ssssay so. But would you mind putting those opposable thumbs of yours to good use and *get meow-t of here!*"

Penny and Luke jumped into action. Luke tore off the cardboard and stood aside when Mo pounced on the bed. Penny's fingers were shaking so badly she couldn't get the bonnet strings untied.

"Rip it off, before that girl gets back here," Mo told her.

As soon as Penny and Luke had stripped Mo, the cat smoothed the fur on his back where the doll clothes had been.

"This is impossible," Penny said. "Does Mr. Leery know you can talk?"

Mo stopped grooming and sighed. "I told him he should tell you everything, but he didn't think you were ready." The more Mo talked, the more human he sounded, as if his tongue and lips were getting the hang of forming words. "Now it's up to me to get us out of this mess."

"Not ready for what?" Luke wanted to know.

"What mess?" Penny asked.

"Can't tell you," Mo said. Before the kids could

argue, Mo glanced at the window. He arched his back and hissed, showing his glistening fangs. Then he leaped from the bed to the windowsill.

"What's wrong, Mo?" Penny asked.

"Who's out there?" Luke asked.

All three stood at the window, peering into Natalie's front yard. Early morning shadows danced across the yard.

"What are you doing?" Natalie asked, coming into the room and holding a camera. "I told you not to touch anything. Why did you take the clothes off Mo? Now I'll have to get him all dressed again for the picture."

"Mo doesn't like to be dressed like a baby," Penny told Natalie.

"How do you know?" Natalie asked.

"He told us," Luke said.

"Shhh," Penny said.

"I knew it!" Natalie said. "I tried to get him to talk all night long, but he refused." She dropped the camera on the bed so she could open her notebook. Then she kneeled in front of Mo. "Talk," she demanded.

Mo stared at Natalie.

"Say something," Natalie urged.

Mo blinked.

"SAY ANYTHING!" Natalie screamed.

Mo opened his mouth and yawned right in Natalie's face.

"Fine," Natalie said, throwing her notebook on the floor. "If you're going to be that way, then you can all just leave. Now!"

"Gladly," Luke said. He scooped up Mo and followed Penny out of Natalie's house. When they were safely away, Mo curled around Luke's neck as the three made their way back to Mr. Leery's house.

"Nobody is ever going to believe Mo is a talking cat," Luke said.

Penny put her hand on her friend's arm. "Shhh," she warned.

"What's wrong?" Luke asked.

"I've got that feeling again," Penny said. "I think we're being followed."

Mo growled. He glared over Luke's shoulders into the shadows of the thorny bushes and hissed.

5

Mo wouldn't say another word, even though the kids tried all day to get him to talk. The next morning was Monday, so Luke and Penny met at Mr. Leery's before school.

"Come on, Mo," Penny begged. "Talk to us."

Mo just turned his back to them.

"This morning is as bad as last night," Luke complained as they went into Mr. Leery's kitchen.

"What happened to you last night?" Penny asked.

Luke shrugged. "Just stupid little things like my covers getting all tangled. I hate when that happens. Then my pillow disappeared. How can a pillow just vanish? I bet Kendall hid it somewhere."

Kendall was Luke's older sister. She liked to play pranks on Luke. She was a good friend of Mr. Leery's, too.

Penny listened while she gave Mo some water in a yellow bowl. A green feather was on the floor. Penny plucked it up and threw it in the trash can. Mo totally ignored the kids and jumped up onto the kitchen counter to look out the window.

"I hardly got any sleep," Luke said. "And I didn't have any clean underwear so I had to wear the same pair from yesterday."

"Okay," Penny told him. "That is just disgusting."

"Then I went to eat Rice Krispies for breakfast and the milk was spoiled," Luke said. "So far, it's been a rotten day."

Penny gasped. "That is so strange. My neighbor's dog kept barking half the night so I didn't get a single hour of sleep. And I couldn't find two socks that matched this morning."

"Socks don't matter," Luke said.

"Oh yeah?" Penny said. She pulled up her jeans to reveal one bright green sock with purple stripes and another with neon blue flowers.

Luke laughed.

"It's really not funny," Penny told him. "Something weird is going on. My milk was spoiled this morning, too."

"It's just one of those crazy coincidences."

Penny opened Mr. Leery's refrigerator and Luke shook his head. "You shouldn't snoop in other people's stuff," he told her.

Penny didn't listen. She pulled out Mr. Leery's milk and unscrewed the cap.

"Phe-ew!" Luke yelled. "Put the top back on." The horrible smell made Luke gag and hold his nose. Penny quickly put the lid back on and slammed the refrigerator shut.

Both kids looked at Mo.

Penny put her hands on her hips. "Okay, Mo," Penny said firmly. "Tell us what's going on around here."

Mo slowly twisted around and licked his paw. "No need," he said. "I got word from Mr. Leery that he'll be back soon."

"How does a cat get word?" Penny asked him.

"Maybe he has a cell phone," Luke teased. "It's a MeowBerry."

"He'll be here tonight. Now go to school." Mo turned his back to the kids and stared out the window again. "And don't forget to wear your bracelets," he warned.

Penny held her arm up. The old silver bracelet with Mr. Leery's key dangled in midair. Luke patted his pocket. His bracelet was safely tucked in his pocket. There was no way he was wearing that thing to school.

"Come on," Luke said. "If we don't get to school soon, I won't have time to play basketball before the bell rings."

"Oh, all right," Penny said. "But when Mr. Leery gets back, he has a lot of explaining to do."

Luke and Penny jogged the five blocks to school with their backpacks bouncing on their backs. Penny couldn't help glancing over her shoulder every now and then. She still had the feeling that someone was watching her. It was probably just nosy Natalie, but with all the strange things going on, like Mo talking, Penny wasn't sure of anything.

"For crying out loud," Luke said as they trotted onto the school yard. "There's that wild boy from the other day."

Standing on the steps of the school stood the bucktoothed boy with big ears they'd met on Mr. Leery's porch. Penny felt a cold shiver run down her back as she nudged Luke. "That boy is wearing the exact same clothes you wore when we met him."

Luke smiled as they dropped their backpacks in the pile beside the steps. "Well, what can I say?

I have good taste. You think he's wearing dirty underwear, too?"

"Very funny," Penny said.

Luke pulled a small basketball out of his backpack. "Want to play ball?"

Penny shook her head and Luke ran off to the basketball courts. Penny decided to do some spying of her own. She watched the strange boy as he went up to different kids. He stood beside some first graders on the swings.

"Look out!" one kid yelled as he swung higher and higher. "I'm blasting off into outer space."

The strange boy bent down and put his hands over his head. Nobody but Penny noticed. Then the boy slinked over to some sixth-grade girls. They stood in a circle, giggling and talking about boys. The weird kid tried to get in the middle of the circle, but the girls were squeezed together tight. The boy dropped to his knees and tried to crawl in. He bumped into one girl's legs and then another. Then he bumped into Thelma Martin.

Nobody messed with Thelma, but this boy didn't know that.

Thelma turned around and grabbed the boy by his ear. "I'm going to turn you into chopped liver!" Thelma yelled.

"No!" squealed the boy. "Not meat. Anything but meat!"

The other girls in the group laughed and Thelma shoved the kid to the ground. "Get lost," she told him.

"But where should I go?" he asked.

Thelma just rolled her eyes and turned back to her friends. Penny wished she had a pink notebook like Natalie's to write all this stuff down. Luke would definitely think something strange was going on when he heard about this.

Penny shoved her hair out of her face. It had gotten so tangled last night; she could hardly get a brush through it this morning. Her hand was still in her hair when someone grabbed her arm.

"Give me that bracelet!" a voice demanded.

6

"Ouch!" Penny yelled. "Leave me alone. You're hurting me."

"I want to see the designs on that bracelet. It looks like something in my father's collection," Natalie told her.

"It's mine," Penny said, pulling her arm away.

"I just wanted to see it again," Natalie said. "You don't have to get so snotty."

Natalie showed off something new practically every day. For once, Penny had something that Natalie didn't have, but for some reason Penny felt the need to keep it a secret. She pushed the bracelet up under her shirtsleeve and turned away from Natalie.

Penny watched the new boy again. He stood beside the basketball hoop, watching Luke and his friends play.

"Why are you watching Bobby?" Natalie asked.

"Who's Bobby?" Penny asked, being sure to still cover her bracelet with her sleeve.

Natalie nodded toward the strange boy. "He's that new kid. There's something funny about him. I've been taking notes." She held up her notebook. "I'm keeping my eye on him."

Penny hated to agree with Natalie about anything, but she had to admit that Bobby wasn't ordinary. When Thomas smacked the ball down on a rebound he yelled "Duck!" to Bobby. But the new kid didn't move out of the way. Instead, he stared into the sky and got whacked on the nose by the ball.

Splat! Bobby slammed to the ground. The boys gathered around Bobby and the playground duty teacher came running. Penny thought she was the only one who noticed that Luke's bracelet had fallen out of his pocket, but Penny was wrong.

Natalie slammed her notebook shut and took off running. Luckily, Penny was faster. She raced ahead of Natalie and grabbed the bracelet off the ground before anyone else saw it. Natalie stomped away in a huff.

In the middle of the crowd of boys, Penny saw Bobby. For a moment, she was afraid he had seen the bracelet. He gave her the meanest look anyone had ever given her. But then he was smiling and saying "I'm fine" to the teacher.

Penny shook her head. Had she imagined the evil look? She wasn't sure, but she was going to be watching Bobby, too. Just like Natalie.

Luke poked her in the side. "Did you see that new kid get slammed? Thomas tried to warn him. I bet his nose swells up to the size of a watermelon."

"His name is Bobby," Penny told Luke. "Natalie is spying on him."

"What else is new?"

"I'm spying on him, too," Penny said.

Luke laughed and looked at Penny. "Are you turning into a Natalie clone?"

Penny shook her head. "No, but you have to admit that kid is weird."

"Aren't you the one who's always saying people can't help it if their ears are big or their legs are skinny?" Luke asked.

"Yeah," Penny said, "but that's not it. He gave me this awful look."

"You mean like this?" Luke asked. He stuck his tongue out, pulled his eyes sideways and scrunched up his nose.

"Ha, ha," Penny said as the bell rang to start the school day. Luke ran off to get in line, but Penny frowned. Thomas and Alex lifted Bobby off the ground and helped him to the door. Luke grabbed their backpacks and followed them into the building.

"Okay, class. Turn in your homework," Mr.

Crandle, their fifth-grade teacher, told them the minute they walked in the classroom door.

Penny pulled her homework out of her bag. Or at least she tried to. It wasn't there. "What happened to my homework?" she asked herself.

Penny shook everything out of her book bag. Her lunch, notebook, and pencils tumbled out. She searched through her notebook, but found nothing.

"Now, I'm in trouble," Penny mumbled to herself.

"Who took my homework?" Natalie yelled. "I know it was in here." She dumped the contents of her book bag onto her desk. A calculator, a cell phone, a makeup kit, a brush, comb, pink pencils and pens, and two brand-new pink notebooks tumbled out.

All across the room, girls searched in their backpacks, but none of them could find their homework. For once, every boy handed in his homework.

Mr. Crandle stood at the front of the room, tapping his foot. "Girls," he said. "Is this some kind of joke?"

Natalie pointed at Thomas. "The boys must have stolen our homework!" she shrieked.

Natalie always had her homework turned in on time and she rarely ever got a question wrong. If Penny's homework hadn't been missing too, she would have loved seeing Natalie so upset.

"Nonsense," Mr. Crandle told her. "The girls must be trying to get the boys in trouble."

"Yeah," Luke said. "We didn't do anything. We were playing basketball this morning. Just ask him."

Luke pointed to the door where Bobby stood with the principal. "Excuse me," said Mrs. Bender, the principal. "You have a new student."

Bobby took a big red apple out of his pocket and handed it to Mr. Crandle. "Oh brother," Alex muttered. "Another teacher's pet."

Bobby looked at Alex and then at Mr. Crandle. Luke couldn't believe what Bobby did next. He actually petted Mr. Crandle on the arm. Mr. Crandle snatched his arm away. He pointed to a seat by Natalie. "You may sit there."

Penny hoped that Bobby's strange behavior would make Mr. Crandle forget about the missing homework, but no such luck. At recess time, Mr. Crandle cleared his throat and said, "Girls, you will stay inside and finish your homework. And no more jokes tomorrow."

The girls groaned, but the boys raced outside. Penny watched out the window as Bobby followed Alex around like a puppy. Finally, Alex must have told him to quit it because then Bobby patted Thomas on the arm. Thomas shoved Bobby away. Bobby tumbled to the ground and rolled over backward. Penny had never seen a kid so clumsy. Even when he walked, he tripped over his own feet.

When Bobby got up, he stumbled into Luke.

When Luke handed Bobby the ball, Bobby sniffed it and then dropped it, not even bothering to notice where it bounced.

"Oh, Penny," Mr. Crandle said. "Please give this to Mr. Leery. He lent it to me last week. Tell him it was fascinating."

"Sure," Penny said. She looked at the book Mr. Crandle put on her desk. It was called *History of Ancient Civilizations*. Nothing sounded more boring to Penny, but she knew Mr. Crandle and Mr. Leery both belonged to the History Club at the Morgantown Library. A bunch of senior citizens got together at the History Club once a week, talked about old stuff, and ate pizza. Penny's grandmother had told her about it. Penny smiled. She knew her grandmother had a crush on Mr. Leery.

For the rest of the school day, Penny noticed that Bobby sneaked up behind everyone but her to sniff them. He sniffed hair. He sniffed books. She even saw him sniffing baseball caps and book bags. She was glad he kept his distance, but she wondered why he didn't like her. She even smelled her armpits to make sure she didn't stink.

At lunch, Luke told Penny that the new kid would be walking home with them. "Does he live close to us?" Penny asked. She didn't remember any houses being for sale on her block.

Luke shrugged. "I guess so."

After school, Penny remembered Luke's bracelet was still in her pocket. "Here," she told him as everyone grabbed their backpacks. "Put this on. It fell out of your pocket this morning."

Luke's face turned red. He quickly grabbed the bracelet and stuffed it in his pocket. "Don't let anyone see that," he said. "It's girly."

"No, it's not," Penny told him. "I saw Carl Anthony wearing something like it one time on TV."

"Really?" Luke said. Carl Anthony was Luke's favorite professional ballplayer.

"Just put it on before you lose it again," Penny told him.

Luke snapped the bracelet on his wrist, but he still pulled his sleeve down to cover it. He wasn't so sure Thomas or the other guys would think it was cool.

Penny and Luke walked out of school and stood beside the Morgantown Elementary School sign to wait for Bobby. They waved as the rest of their friends ran down the sidewalk. They waited and waited and waited some more until the side-walks were completely empty. "Where is he?" Penny asked.

"Maybe his mother picked him up," Luke said.

"I never saw his mother or father this morning, did you?" Penny asked.

Luke shook his head no. "Come on, let's go home," he said. "Bobby's not coming." The two kids walked down the sidewalk. A cool breeze blew some leftover autumn leaves across their path.

"Don't you think it's odd that Bobby came to school all by himself on his first day?" Penny asked.

"I guess so," Luke said. "Maybe his parents are weird, too."

The bracelet on her arm felt warm and the most peculiar idea popped into her head.

"Maybe he doesn't have parents," Penny said. "Maybe he's not a kid."

Luke laughed. "That's the skinniest grown-up I've ever seen."

Suddenly, Luke scratched his arm beside his bracelet. "Did this thing just get hot?"

Penny nodded. "Remember how Mr. Leery told us these bracelets are for protection?" she said slowly.

"I think he just wanted us to be sure not to lose them," Luke said.

"Maybe it's more than that." Penny stopped walking and pulled up her sleeve so she could see the silver on her arm. Even though the bracelet sparkled in the warm sun, a cold chill sent goose bumps racing up her neck.

"There's something weird going on in this town," Penny said. "And I think we better wear these bracelets every single minute until we get some answers."

7

"Tell us what's wrong, Mo," Penny pleaded.

"We know you can," Luke added.

Penny and Luke had stopped by Mr. Leery's house. If anyone could tell them what was going on it was the talking cat. Mo was so restless they took him to Luke's house, hoping the change of scenery would calm him down. No such luck.

The black cat remained silent. He padded nervously around Luke's room, jumping from window to bed to desk to bookshelves and back to the window to peer out into the shadows. His big paws scattered papers and books, but the cat didn't seem to notice. He sat with his nose pressed to the window and his ears perked at attention.

"What's out there?" Luke said. When he walked across the room to look out the window, Mo went into action as if a ghost had pulled his tail. He leaped onto Luke's chest. Luke fell back on the bed, the cat perched on his chest like a lion getting ready for the kill.

Mo pulled back his lips and hissed. "Sssstay away from the window."

Facing the cat's glistening teeth made Luke's face go pale. "W–w–why?"

Mo plopped down on Luke's stomach. "Can't tell," Mo said. He glanced out the window again. A single claw escaped and poked Luke in the stomach.

"Um . . . ouch?" Luke said.

Mo looked back at the boy as if he'd forgotten Luke was there. "Oh. Ssssorry about that."

"Something is obviously wrong," Penny said. "Why won't you tell us?"

"Sssomething is very wrong," Mo said. "But only Leery is allowed to tell you. Until he gets back, you must stay safe."

"Safe from what?" Luke asked, finally getting up enough nerve to push Mo off his stomach.

Mo pounced across the room and landed on top of Luke's desk. "Leery knows. Leery will tell you."

"But Mr. Leery isn't here!" Penny screamed at the cat.

"He will be. Soon," Mo said. "Very soon."

"How do you know that?" Luke asked. "Mr. Leery said he wouldn't be home until tomorrow."

Mo looked at Luke. The cat's amber eyes were wide and unblinking.

"I know. That's all," Mo finally said. Then he went back to looking out the window, his tail lashing from side to side, swiping homework papers to the floor.

The door flew open and Kendall, Luke's older sister, barged into the room.

"Haven't you ever heard of knocking?" Luke asked.

Kendall's eyes grew wide. "I'm going to tell Mom and Dad you have a cat in here."

"This is not just any cat. It's Mo," Penny told her. "We're taking care of him while Mr. Leery is gone."

"Why didn't Mr. Leery ask me?" Kendall said, clearly hurt. "He likes me better than you."

Luke was glad to have the chance to tease his sister. "I guess not."

"That's what you think." Kendall slammed the door on her way out of Luke's room.

Mo sprang off the desk and landed right in front of the bedroom door. "Got to go. Now. I hate doorknobs."

Penny stood in front of the door, her hands on her hips, and met Mo's eyes with a glare of her own. "I'm not opening this door until you spill the beans."

"Do you really think that's a good idea?" Luke

said. "I mean, Mo has claws and he's not afraid to use them."

"He wouldn't dare," Penny said. She looked at Mo. "Would you?"

Mo's claws pricked at the carpet and he growled deep in his chest, but Penny didn't back down.

"Okay." Mo sighed. "You win. No. I would not use your leg as a scratching post. But I do need you to move out of the way. Leery's back. He must see you. NOW!"

"How do you know stuff like that?" Luke asked as he grabbed a sweatshirt off the floor and pulled it on.

"You'll find out," Mo said. He swished out the door Penny had just opened.

The two tiny windows next to Mr. Leery's front door glowed with light when Penny and Luke banged on the door.

"We know your cat can talk," Luke blurted as soon as Mr. Leery opened the door. "Are you some kind of magician?"

Penny and Luke stepped inside the warmth of the cottage. Mo ran between their legs and jumped up into Mr. Leery's arms. Penny and Luke didn't realize a cat could purr as loudly as Mo did when he saw Mr. Leery.

Mr. Leery's face was lined with wrinkles deeper than usual. Dark circles underlined his eyes. He held Mo in the crook of his arm and raised his eyebrows at the cat.

"You agreed to keep your mouth shut until I returned," Mr. Leery said.

"I guess I let the cat out of the bag," Mo admitted.

For a moment, the cat's face seemed to dissolve into a look of shame, but then Mo's whiskers twitched and his tail swished back and forth in an angry frenzy. He leaped out of Mr. Leery's arms and rushed to the door, peering between Luke's knees out into the shadows of the yard.

"Quick. Close the door. NOW!" Mo yowled.

Mr. Leery pushed Luke aside and slammed the

door shut, locking it with a silver bolt. He nudged Penny out of the way and dropped the shades on the windows. Then he turned, his robe billowing out like wings, and rushed to the kitchen. Penny and Luke hurried after him. Mr. Leery peered out the back window into his yard. The shadows from the thick bushes bordering their town seemed thicker, blacker. A gray fog swirled on the ground, searching for something to hide.

The fur on Mo's back stood up and his back arched in warning. His tail had puffed up three times its normal size.

Mr. Leery pressed his nose to the glass, trying to make sense out of the shadows in his backyard, but the ground was shrouded in fog. "Is there a leak? Are we in danger?"

"Leak? What kind of leak?" Penny asked.

Luke chimed in. "Danger from what?"

At the sound of their voices, Mr. Leery jumped straight up and banged his head on the window.

"Tell us," Penny told him.

Mr. Leery rubbed his head and glanced out the window, then looked at Mo. "Do we have time?" he asked the cat.

Mo paced back and forth across the kitchen table. "At this point, sooner is definitely better than later," the cat said.

Mr. Leery snapped the kitchen window shade shut and slumped into a chair. "Sit," he said. "This is going to take a while."

And then he began to tell Luke and Penny a very strange story.

8

"This is not a story to be taken lightly," Mr. Leery said as they sat around the table. "Let me start by telling you about the bushes that border this town."

Luke shook his head as if he were shaking spiderwebs from his hair. "Why are you talking about gardening? Who cares about some idiot's idea of landscaping?"

Mr. Leery's face drained of all color. "Those bushes are not there for decoration," he said.

"Of course not. Nobody in their right mind would think a web of thorns is pretty," Penny said. "In fact, they're an eyesore. Someone should chop them all down."

"Are you insane?" the cat shrieked.

"Hush, Mo," Mr. Leery said. "They don't know what they're saying."

Luke jumped up so fast the chair tipped over and crashed to the floor. "You keep talking in riddles," he shouted. "Either tell us or I'm going home."

Mr. Leery righted the chair and gently pulled on Luke's arm. As soon as Luke sat, Mo jumped in Luke's lap to keep the boy still.

"You're right," Mr. Leery said. "The truth is that those are no ordinary bushes and they were not planted by any ordinary person. They are a magical weaving placed by the original Keyholders."

"The original what?" Penny asked.

"Key-hold-ers," Mo repeated for her.

Mr. Leery placed both of his wrinkled hands on the table and leaned forward, looking first at Penny and then at Luke. "That's right. Keyholders.

Three humans whose duty it is to maintain the border between your world and the world of magic."

"Um, could you repeat that?" Luke interrupted. "Only slower? In plain English? So it makes sense?"

"He's talking about the three who keep the world of magic from leaking into your backyard," Mo said.

"Did you say magic?" Penny asked.

"They need to clean out their ears," Mo said to Mr. Leery, taking a swipe at his own with a licked paw.

Luke ignored the cat. "Are you trying to tell us that there's another entire world right on the other side of those bushes?" he asked.

Mr. Leery nodded. "That is why no one ever dares to cross the border. It is forbidden. But there are beings on the other side that desire to break through the border. Keyholders guard the entryways between the magic world and the world you've always known, keeping all safe from an invasion by forces that would destroy us."

"Wait, wait, wait," Penny said. She held up her hands as if warding off a swarm of bees. "Don't say another word. There is no such thing as magic except in the fairy tales that parents read to little kids."

"Where do you think fairy tales came from?" Mr. Leery asked. "Those same stories are based on tales passed down from generation to generation, told by ancestors who once lived side by side with the magical realm. But as with all things, the relationship soured. And that is never a good thing when one is more powerful than the other. If the border had not been formed, the magical realm would have overpowered this real world, and life as we know it would have ceased to exist."

Mr. Leery looked both of them in the eyes before continuing. "Without Keyholders, the magic world could invade this world. And that is why I need you. There are creatures that are tired of being banished on the far side of the border. They plan to invade this world and take it as their very own."

"So what?" Luke said. "Wouldn't having flying monkeys and little fairies flitting around be sort of fun?"

Mr. Leery gasped. "Oh, my my my, no," he muttered. "Understand this. I speak not of the cute little beings from beddy-bye-time fairy tales. Oh yes, there are those, too. But there are also the big and the powerful and the ferocious. The beings from which monster stories come."

"Monsters?" Penny squeaked.

"You know. Like ogres and trolls and ghouls," Mo said matter-of-factly.

Luke gulped. "Um. Maybe we better find one of those Keyholders and make sure they're doing their job."

"I am doing my best," Mr. Leery said.

"You?" Penny and Luke gasped at the same time.

Mr. Leery seemed to deflate like a balloon. "Yes. Me. I am the last Keyholder of three," he said. "I just returned from the funeral of the next-to-the-last Keyholder. The first died nearly 100 years ago."

"What about Mo?" Penny said. "Isn't he a Keyholder?"

Mo made a sound as if he were hacking up a hairball the size of Tennessee. "Do I *look* like a humdrum?" he spat and jumped onto the table.

"A what?" Penny asked.

Mr. Leery answered for Mo. "Humdrum is what the magical realm calls those of us that live on this side of the border. Those who possess no extraordinary powers. Keyholders must be born of the humdrums, though they might have ancestral blood from the lands beyond the border. Obviously, Mo is not from this side. He is my link."

"Link?" Luke stood up from the table and shook his head, trying to make sense of it all.

Mr. Leery wearily shook his head. "There is so much to teach. And we have such little time," he muttered. Then he sat up a bit straighter. "Links are beings from beyond the border that form a special connection to the Keyholders. It's a bond that lasts a lifetime. Mo is my link. We are inseparable."

Luke snorted. "Now I know you're pulling our legs because you just left Mo for days!"

"And I wasn't very happy about it, either," Mo said with a growl.

"It couldn't be helped," Mr. Leery explained. "These are unusual times, for new Keyholders must be chosen. And that only occurs every two hundred years."

"But that would mean that you're over two hundred years old," Penny said.

Mr. Leery nodded. "Actually, I'm two hundred and sixty years old."

This time Luke laughed out loud. "You don't look a day over a hundred!"

Penny put a hand on Luke's arm. "He's not joking."

"But we've known you all our lives," Luke argued.

Mr. Leery nodded. "And I've been watching you all of your lives. *You* are my chosen apprentices."

Luke and Penny stared at Mr. Leery as if he'd sprouted wings and was going to fly away.

Penny shook her head. "That's too bad because there's no way I'm going to become some two-hundred-year-old Keynut."

"That's Keyholder," Luke corrected.

"Well, you can forget the whole crazy thing. I have things to do—like study for my math test." She stood, ready to march straight out the front door, but a noise at the window stopped her dead in her tracks.

Mr. Leery dived across the table and grabbed Penny's arm.

"What are you doing?" She tried to pull away,

but Mr. Leery dug his bony fingers around her wrist. "Your bracelet. Where is it?" he asked.

"It's right here," Penny said, shaking her arm until the bracelet slipped loose from her shirtsleeve.

"What about yours?" Mr. Leery asked, turning to Luke and eyeing his bare wrists. "Where is it?"

Luke stepped back. "Don't get your underwear tied in a knot," he said, digging into his pocket and pulling out the silver band with the key dangling from it. "It's right here.

"Put it on. Quickly!" Mr. Leery cried out. Then he held out his own wrist so the two friends could see his battered band of silver. A small purple stone was set into the metal.

"Hey," Luke said. "That looks just like Mo's collar."

"This is the band of a Keyholder," Mr. Leery told them. "We are linked by stone and spirit."

Penny looked at the key dangling from her bracelet. "You mean, this is the key to a magic land?"

"Oh, brother," Mo huffed. "This is not going well."

"Hush, Mo," Mr. Leery said before answering Penny's question. "That, my dear, is the key to my home. You have much to learn before I can entrust you with magical keys. The band itself is what links Keyholders together. This last bracelet I will give to the last Keyholder apprentice. It is more than just a pretty bauble. The silver was forged beyond the border, cast with magic intended to aid us in our work by protecting us from those that mean us harm. And one of the most important things it does is to protect us from boggarts."

"Did you say boogers?" Luke asked.

"Boggarts," Mr. Leery repeated, and then explained about the creatures.

"They're creatures of magic, scared off by the sounds of bells and the glint of silver. The Queen of Boggarts has strong magic, and she has been getting restless. In fact, I'm not so sure she didn't have something to do with the death of the second Keyholder, for if ever the Keyholders are defeated she would have free access across the border. I'm convinced she will send a spy to find out if I've chosen new apprentices."

"Spy?" Luke squeaked.

"What, exactly, would this boggart spy look like?" Penny asked. "It wouldn't happen to have blond pigtails, a pink notebook, and live in the biggest house in town, would it?"

Mr. Leery blinked his eyes in confusion. "Of course not. Boggarts are truly ugly creatures with ears that stick out and knobby knees that make them very clumsy."

"That eliminates Natalie," Luke told Penny. "She doesn't have big ears. Just a big mouth."

"Of course it's not Natalie," Mr. Leery said. "But don't go looking for a creature that sticks out like a sore thumb. Boggarts are chameleons. They change their shape, blending with their environment over time so as not to be noticed. They're not really good spies; mostly they like to cause trouble and play tricks. Milk curdles when they're nearby and animals detest them. Important documents just disappear."

"Important documents?" Penny repeated. "Like homework?"

"I suppose so," Mr. Leery said distractedly. "That's why I left Mo here with you. It's painful to be separated from a link, but Mo can detect a boggart spy."

"Their smell is atrocious," Mo said with a nod.

Penny gasped. Luke fell in a chair.

"Uh-oh," Luke said. "I think the boggart spy has already been here."

They told Mr. Leery about the kid who kept following them.

"But Bobby really stuck out," Luke argued. "Because he was wearing a pink tutu."

"Only at first," Penny added. "The next day he wore clothes identical to what you had on."

"Yes, yes," Mr. Leery said. "That had to be

him. Boggarts change as necessary to blend in. He must not have known what to wear at first, but when he saw you he was fast to change."

The words were barely out of his mouth when Mr. Leery grabbed Mo and held him up so he could look straight into his link's face. "Is it true?" he asked. "Has the spy arrived?"

Mo's tail swished violently from side to side. "I told you. I keep getting a whiff of a stinking boggart," the cat said. "It comes and goes. The spy must have slipped through the border, but he hasn't figured out who Penny and Luke really are. At least, not yet."

Mr. Leery tucked Mo under his arm and rushed to the front door. Mr. Leery slid back the silver latch and opened the door just a crack so he could peer into the black night. "He could be getting close. Too close. He must be stopped."

Mr. Leery released Mo into the black night. "It all depends on you, Mo. Get him!"

"No!!!!" Penny screamed. "Mo might get hurt."

She rushed toward the door, but Mr. Leery slammed it shut and flipped the silver latch closed.

"Aren't you worried that the boggart might think cats make tasty little snacks?" Luke asked.

"Cat? What cat?"

"Um . . . *your* cat," Luke said. "The one you just sent out into the night to do battle with an evil magical creature. That one."

"Mo? Oh. No, no, no. I'm not concerned about Mo. If Mo finds that spy, it is the spy who will be in trouble," Mr. Leery said, but the next words he spoke sent shivers racing up Penny's and Luke's spines.

"But if Mo fails, we all must worry. Every last one of us."

9

Luke jammed his hands over his ears. "What's making that horrible noise?"

"Don't worry," Mr. Leery told them. "It's only the boggart."

Penny pulled open the shade on a front window. "What if that's Mo screaming? We should help him."

Mr. Leery shook his head. "Mo doesn't need our help."

Another screech came from the front yard. Penny couldn't take it anymore. She had to help Mo. After all, he was just a defenseless spotted cat. She flung open the door and rushed outside.

"Wait!" yelled Mr. Leery, but Penny was already in the yard. She rushed to protect Mo, but skidded to a stop.

An enormous spotted panther held Bobby down on the ground with a massive black paw. Huge white fangs glistened as the panther's mouth opened wide over Bobby's neck. The boy squirmed and squealed, "Help me."

"Mr. Leery, hurry. A monster is eating Bobby," Penny screamed.

Mr. Leery ran out onto the porch. "That's no monster. That's Mo."

"Mo?" Luke gulped.

Mo looked up from the boy for just a second, but it was all the time Bobby needed. He jumped up, knocked Mo to the ground, and leaped into a huge tree.

"How did he do that?" Penny asked. No normal kid could jump that high. There was no way a boy could push off a huge panther, either.

But Bobby wasn't normal. In front of their eyes, he changed from being a scrawny kid into an ugly ape-like creature with pointed ears and yellow eyes. He got bigger and bigger until the tree branch groaned under his weight.

He cackled and pointed to Mr. Leery. "I know your secret. I know your secret!"

Before Penny could blink, the ape-boy laughed wickedly and swung from tree branch to tree branch toward the woods.

Mo growled and leaped into the air. As he soared over the ground, wings unfurled from his back and he flew after Bobby.

"Get him, Mo!" shouted Mr. Leery.

Suddenly, the gray fog swirled up from the ground and swallowed Bobby. Mo flew around and around, but the boy had disappeared.

Penny's legs shook. Her stomach felt like snakes were wiggling inside her. "Did I just see Mo fly and Bobby turn into some kind of ape?"

"No, of course not," Mr. Leery told her.

"Oh good," she said. Maybe the fog had made her see things.

"That boy turned into a boggart. He was the spy I feared." Mr. Leery waved his hand and Mo immediately flew to his side.

Luke stared at the spot where Bobby had disappeared. "Where did he? . . . How did he? . . ."

"He just vanished!" Penny said in amazement. She ran through the fog to right below where Bobby had been, but he wasn't there.

Mr. Leery shook his head. "This is not good. Not good at all."

"And Mo. He's not an ordinary cat. He's . . . he's . . ." Luke turned to look at Mo, but Mo was a small cat with a spotted belly again, licking his paw. Luke's head suddenly hurt. Was he asleep and having a bad dream?

"This is real, isn't it?" Penny said.

"As real as homework," Mo told her before licking his paw again. "If you hadn't stopped me, our troubles would be over."

"But I couldn't let you hurt Bobby," Penny said.

Mo turned his back to her. "You have much to learn."

Mr. Leery rubbed his bald head. "Oh dear. Oh dear. The Boggart Queen will soon know that I have chosen you as my apprentices. What to do? What to do?"

Mo growled. "It can't be helped. We'll have to hurry."

"Of course," Mr. Leery said, swirling around and rushing to his house.

"Hurry with what?" Luke asked.

Mr. Leery paused. "Why, the installation ceremony, of course."

"Whoa, let's wait just a minute," Penny said, holding up a hand. "This sounds crazy."

"Besides, I thought you needed three Keyholders," Luke said.

Mr. Leery nodded. "We do, but we haven't time. I will stand in place of the third for now." He looked up in the sky before adding. "If one boggart can get through, then more will soon follow."

Penny shivered. "More of what?" she asked. But she already knew the answer. She definitely didn't like the idea of hairy, yellow-eyed monsters running around Morgantown doing whatever they wanted.

Mr. Leery grabbed his walking stick from inside the house and walked toward the web of thorny bushes that bordered their town. With every step Penny and Luke felt fluttering in their stomachs.

"We can't go in there," Luke warned. "We're not allowed."

"It can't be helped," Mr. Leery said. "Don't worry. Mo will protect us and you have your bracelets."

"Quickly," Mo said. "I sent word. The ceremony must begin now."

Luke laughed. "Mo must be using his cat cell phone again."

Mr. Leery lifted his walking stick. Immediately, the thick bushes and tangled vines of the woods parted like they'd been cut by a knife. A glow from the end of the stick lit up the way.

Penny held her stomach and hoped she wouldn't throw up. "Wait. This is like a dream I had once."

Luke's head pounded and he suddenly remembered. "I've had a dream like this every year on my birthday."

"And now is the time for the dream to come true," Mo purred.

Penny shook her head. "No, I'm not becoming a Keyholder until I'm old enough to drive. Maybe not ever!"

Luke put his arm around Penny. "Mr. Leery would never do anything to hurt us. He's babysat us all our lives. I think he's telling us the truth."

Penny knew that Mo and Mr. Leery were telling the truth, but she wasn't sure if she could do it. She always planned everything. She made her school lunch the night before and even laid her clothes out on her chair so she'd be ready faster in the morning. Her birthday wasn't for four months, but she had already written out the invitations to the party. Being a Keyholder had never entered into any of her plans.

"If we don't like being Keyholders, can we quit?" she asked.

Mr. Leery dropped his walking stick down to his side. Immediately the bushes, trees, and vines wove back together.

In the faint light, Penny saw Mr. Leery's face soften. He placed a hand on her shoulder. "I'm sorry this happened the way it did. I didn't mean to frighten you. Being a Keyholder is a choice and one that can be changed. It's a lot to ask of a ten-year-old."

Penny chewed on her lip and thought about her family. She pictured her home and how secure she had always felt there. Now she knew if the Keyholders failed, her world would change.

More boggarts, and creatures even worse, would change everything. She'd never be safe again. Neither would her family.

Penny had known Mr. Leery all her life. He had been a babysitter and friend. When she'd had chicken pox, he had stayed home with her when her mother had to work. She had always trusted him. Always. She couldn't stop now—now that he needed her to help him. "Okay," Penny finally said. "My mom always told me I'd be somebody great someday. I just didn't know it'd be today. I'm ready."

Mr. Leery nodded and put his right hand on Luke's shoulder. "And you?" Mr. Leery asked. "Are you ready?"

Luke took a deep breath and stood up tall. Penny held her breath. She knew she couldn't be a Keyholder without Luke's help. Luke smiled, and Penny was afraid he would make a joke, but then Luke's smile faded and he had never looked more serious. "Let's save the world."

10

The woods opened up and swallowed them whole. That's how it seemed to Luke. When he looked back, the bushes and vines closed in darkness behind them, so he kept his eyes on the light and parting trees ahead of him.

"This is the first time we've ever been in here," Penny said in a hushed voice. She wasn't sure why she whispered, but for some reason she did.

"I know," Mr. Leery said softly. "It's very rare for anyone from the humdrum world to be here."

"It's not as creepy as I thought," Luke said.

He spoke too soon. A rustling in the bushes

made him jump. Shadows moved around them and strange noises filled the night. Luke got the feeling they were being surrounded. He grabbed a stick from the ground, just in case wild animals jumped at them.

Penny was startled by an entire colony of fireflies swarming in front of her face. She shook her head, but one still landed on her nose. Then she saw it wasn't a firefly at all. A miniature person with golden wings and blue skin stared up at her. "It's a tiny fairy," Penny said breathlessly.

Luke pointed to a clearing in front of them that filled up with short, rather fat people with pointy ears. "I think those are elves."

The oldest-looking of the elves approached Luke and swatted his finger. "It's not polite to point."

Mr. Leery cleared his throat. "So sorry, Bridger. We have no time for pleasantries. The hour is upon us."

Mr. Leery poked his walking stick into the

ground and the area around them glowed with a buttery yellow light. The shadows that Luke had sensed became real beings, but nothing like any the kids had ever seen before.

Elf-like creatures with long skinny legs stared at Luke. Young girls with violet skin and hair of flowers and leaves pressed close to Penny. They moved like dancers. Penny felt big and awkward beside them. A half man–half horse moved out from behind a clump of bushes. A tall green man with leaves for hands could almost be mistaken for a tree. So many creatures filled the area around the kids, Penny couldn't keep up with them all. Just when Luke thought there couldn't be any more, there were.

A swirling blaze roared up out of the ground beside Mr. Leery. It became a large bald-headed man wearing only gold baggy pants. Three thin women whose bodies seemed to glow floated down from the treetops near a huddle of men wearing robes of many different colors. A loud clap of thunder made Penny look up to see if it was going to rain, but she only saw wings flying through a misty cloud.

The young girls draped flowers on Penny's and Luke's heads and necks. "Thank you," Luke said, but the girls only giggled as their eyes blazed a bright blue.

"Are you . . . nymphs?" Penny asked. When they had studied mythology earlier in the school year, she had looked at a picture of beautiful girls like these. But the nymphs danced away as a large animal burst into the clearing.

Penny gasped. It was a pure white unicorn the size of a Shetland pony. It stared at Penny with liquid blue eyes before rearing up on its hind legs and tossing its long white mane. A silver collar, complete with an emerald that matched Penny's, hung around the unicorn's neck.

Penny suddenly felt at peace with the world, as if a warm blanket had engulfed her mind. Every-thing was good and as it should be. How could anything be wrong when such a glorious creature existed? The silver horn spiraled upward toward the sky, but when the creature opened its mouth Penny's peaceful spell was broken.

"It's about time!" the unicorn snapped in a voice that sounded like one of Kendall's snotty teenage friends.

Luke laughed. "You can talk, too?"

The unicorn snorted. "Of course. I've been waiting here for, like, forever. What took you so long? Don't you think I have better things to do than wait on you? Don't you know we need to hurry?"

"I—I didn't know," Penny stammered.

Mr. Leery took Penny's hand and laid it on the unicorn's large white nose. It felt softer than anything Penny had ever touched, even the velvet dress she'd gotten for Christmas. "Penny, this is Kirin."

Kirin nuzzled Penny's hand, filling it with a warm whiff of breath. Penny couldn't imagine an animal more beautiful. Kirin leaned against Penny and Penny instinctively looped her arm over the unicorn's neck. Kirin's scent was like sweet wild-flowers.

A loud burp rang through the trees above the kids. A flash of light and warmth filled the air over them. Luke looked up in time to see fire come out of the mouth of a green bird the size of a Dober-man pinscher. It only took him a moment to figure out that the large scaled creature that swooped down to land in front of him was no bird.

"It's a dragon!" Luke exclaimed.

Kirin snorted. "You picked a smart one there, Leery."

Luke's cheeks burned. Obviously, the animal was a dragon, but it wasn't like he'd ever seen one before. It wasn't as if they even existed. None of these things were supposed to be happening.

The dragon burped again and flames shot out of his nose, roasting a small bush. "I'll take him," the dragon said.

Mr. Leery nodded. "Thank you, Dracula."

"Dracula?" Luke gulped and put his hands over his neck, but then Dracula plopped down on the ground in front of Luke. A silver collar with a single red stone sparkled on the dragon's neck. Luke looked at his bracelet and for the first time noticed it had a garnet, too.

"Scratch my chin! Scratch my chin!" the dragon said, holding his head up to show a line of bright blue scales. Luke couldn't help but grin. The scales were softer than Luke thought they'd be. Dracula's tail thumped on the ground, and the dragon gurgled with delight. When the dragon looked deep into Luke's eyes, Luke felt a tickle in his brain.

"That settles it," Mr. Leery told them. "You have been accepted by the magical world."

"We have?" Penny said.

"Oh, yes. Only those who are accepted by a link can be chosen as Keyholders."

Mo leaped into Mr. Leery's arms. "I am Evan Leery's link. I chose him two hundred years ago. Behold your own links for life."

Luke reached out his hand to touch Dracula again. Luke's hand was almost to the green scaly nose when Dracula reared back and let out a large sneeze. Dragon snot flew onto Luke.

"Sorry about that," Dracula said as Luke stood dripping in bright orange goo.

"Oh, for heavens sake," Kirin snapped. "Will you please stop eating wild turkberries? You know you're allergic."

Kirin tapped Dracula's nose once with her spiraled horn. Immediately, Dracula's red nose turned green.

"Wow, how did you do that?" Luke asked.

Kirin huffed. "I'm a unicorn. Unicorns can heal. Don't you know anything?"

"Thanks," Dracula told Kirin.

"You'd better be more careful. You could have burned him to ashes and then where would we be?" Kirin shook her thick white mane out of her eyes and stepped beside Penny.

"Let's begin, then," Mr. Leery said. A large group of men wearing different colored robes stepped forward along with the three thin women. They raised their hands over the kids.

"Excuse me," Luke said as he wiped orange dragon snot off his face. "Could I have a little help here? Does anyone have a towel?"

The old elf called Bridger chuckled. "Not to worry. Dragon snot won't hurt you. In fact, some say it has magical powers."

Luke shrugged and let the goo drip off his chin. Dracula took his place beside Luke.

Music came from the fluttering wings of the fairies. The fairies sang with such lovely voices that Penny felt like crying.

"Centuries pass like a day;
New Keyholders look our way.
Keep our worlds free from those who roam;
Let all within each find a happy home."

The fairies sang the song over and over. The nymphs tossed green leaves and flowers over Penny's and Luke's head as magical creatures

walked or flew by. Each sang along with the nymphs. Penny's eyes misted over at the beauty of it all. It seemed like hours until every elf, centaur, wizard, and unidentified creature had waved their hands over Penny and Luke.

Finally, Mr. Leery cleared his throat and said, "It is done."

Penny looked at Luke and burst out laughing. He had green leaves and purple flowers plastered all over the orange dragon snot on his body.

"You're a mess," she told him.

Luke shook his head and reached out to touch a scale on Dracula's wing. "No, I'm a Keyholder. And that is a huge responsibility. But I'm ready."

The smile faded from her face as she realized Luke was right. "Now what happens?" she asked softly.

11

Kirin butted Penny gently in the behind with her forehead. "Move it, would ya? It's not like I have all night, you know. I need my midnight snack."

Penny lurched through the bushes and fell into Mr. Leery's backyard. Kirin leaped over her with a snort. Luke tripped over Penny and fell on the ground next to her as Dracula flew through the gaping hole in the bushes. Dracula had a strand of pink berries in his mouth. He settled next to a tall oak tree and crunched the berries with big pointed teeth.

As soon as Mr. Leery stepped into his yard, he waved his walking stick at the bushes. The giant thorns clicked and clacked like deadly knitting needles as they weaved back into place, the web that would keep the world of the humdrums separate from the world of magic.

Kirin tugged up grass and chewed it while the bushes finished their work.

Dracula hiccupped and shot a stream of fire across Mr. Leery's yard. A forsythia bush burst into flame. "Oops," said the dragon.

Kirin swished her tail over the flames, putting out the fire, but the bush collapsed into a pile of ash.

"How in the world are we supposed to hide a unicorn and a dragon?" Penny asked Mr. Leery.

"Yeah. What happens if Dracula sets fire to the school?" Luke added. He smiled and looked at his link. "Could you really do that?"

"Luke!" Penny snapped. "You are not going to burn down the school."

"But we have that math test on Friday," Luke reminded her.

"No," Penny said firmly. "But what *are* we going to do with our links?" she asked. "It's not like a unicorn and a dragon can just blend in."

Luke agreed. "You have it easy. Mo is just an ordinary cat."

Luke had obviously said the wrong thing. Mo hissed. He bristled. He began to grow and grow. His back legs morphed into lion claws, his front legs into a raptor's talons. Whiskers curled and melded into a razor-sharp beak and wings sprouting bright feathers unfurled from his sides. The tuft of fur between his ears became a golden crest. What had once been Mo, glared down at Luke as if he were a pile of fresh hamburger.

"Oh dear, oh dear, oh dear," Mr. Leery said. "There is nothing ordinary about a shape-shifter, especially when his original form happens to be a griffin. They are majestic and vigilant creatures sworn to protect and defend us all against evil.

But they are a little proud. Please say you're sorry."

Luke stuttered an apology and Mo shrank before their eyes until he was once again a cat. A lone purple feather floated through the air and landed on Luke's sneaker. Mo gave Luke one last look and then turned his back on the kids and started smoothing down the tuft of hair between his ears with his paw.

"Are you a shape-shifter, too?" Penny asked Kirin hopefully.

Kirin stopped munching grass. "Why would I want to change shapes? I'm perfect just the way I am."

Dracula spread his wings and flew to the top of a crab apple tree. His weight caused the tree to double over until it rested on the ground. "Me, too! Me, too! I'm perfect, too!" the dragon squawked.

"See?" Penny said to Mr. Leery. "There's no way we can hide them. What are we going to do?"

Luke held out his hand, a grin spreading across

his face. "Maybe we don't want to hide them," he said. "Just think about the looks on the teachers' faces when they see a dragon staring them down. We'd never be sent to the principal's office again!"

"Oh, no no no no," Mr. Leery said. "You cannot let your links be discovered. That could mean the beginning of chaos."

"Then you'll have to figure out a way to hide them," Penny said.

"That's it!" Mr. Leery said. "We'll hide them."

Their neighbor faced the bushes one more time and began to mutter. A faint rustling came from deep within the tangled thorns. The sound grew louder and louder. The bushes trembled and swayed until something finally emerged near Mr. Leery's knees.

Penny gasped. Luke jumped back.

Kirin rolled her eyes. Dracula hopped up and down. "It's Snuffles! It's Snuffles!"

A hairy spider with legs the size of baseball

bats stepped into Mr. Leery's yard. A hundred eyes blinked at Penny and Luke before the arachnid looked back at Mr. Leery.

"I wouldn't ask," Mr. Leery said, "if it wasn't important. But the safety of our world depends on it. Please. Would you?"

The spider named Snuffles rubbed her front two legs together as if she were sharpening knives, but then she heaved a giant sigh and went to work forming silver threads that glistened for the briefest of moments only to seemingly disappear into the night air.

"What is she doing?" Penny asked, still afraid to step closer.

"What all spiders do. Weaving," Mr. Leery said. "But of course, Snuffles is no humdrum spider. She weaves webs of invisibility. They're a tad bit sticky, but they should do the trick. At least until your links learn tricks of their own."

The kids watched as Snuffles' work obliterated a portion of the bushes behind her. "We'll leave her to her work," Mr. Leery said. "By morning there should be a web for both of you to use."

Just then, a rat scurried through the tangle of bushes in the back of the yard.

"Out of my way, out of my way, out of my way," the rat panted as it flitted across the yard and scurried over Mo's paws.

Mo reached out and stopped it with a paw on the rat's tail. The rat squirmed and wiggled, but Mo's paw held firm.

"Let me go, you mangy cat," the rat squealed. "Can't you see? I'm in a hurry!"

Mo licked his chops as Mr. Leery scooped up the rat and carried it inside. "Oh dear, oh dear," Mr. Leery said. "I was afraid of this."

"Afraid of what?" Penny asked. Kirin clomped into the cottage after her, followed by Luke.

Dracula flew in after Luke and landed on a bookcase. Books and wood flew in all directions.

"Oops," Dracula giggled when Mr. Leery eyed the splintered wood with a raised eyebrow.

Mr. Leery closed the door and drew the shades again before speaking. "Three links mean three new Keyholders," Mr. Leery said as he placed the rat on a stool. "I was hoping I could wait to choose the third, but the link is ready. I am out of time."

"You mean a common rat is a link?" Penny asked.

The rat stopped squirming long enough to twitch her whiskers at Penny. "Common? There is nothing common about me. Now, let me go. I have places to go. My link to meet. A world to save!"

Just then there was a knock at the door. Mr. Leery nodded. "That will be the third Keyholder now." He opened the door.

Penny and Luke couldn't believe who it was.

"Wait until I tell my father that this place is infested . . . *infested*, I say, with RATS!" Natalie said, staring at the trembling rat in Mr. Leery's arms.

Penny and Luke stared at each other in horror.

"You have *got* to be kidding," Penny said.

Luke stepped back and bumped into Dracula. "I am *not* going to be a Keyholder with *her*."

Buttercup, the rat, waved at Natalie with one paw. "Got cheese?"

Natalie took one look at the rat and fell over backward. Her legs stuck up in the air like a dead horse. Her pencil and notebook skidded across the floor and landed on Luke's sneaker.

"Here, in this humble cottage, lies the fate of the world as we know it," Mr. Leery said solemnly.

Luke took one look at Natalie. "If we're depending on her to help save the world, then we're in big trouble. Big trouble."

Mo snickered. "For better or worse, it is done. The Keyholders are complete."

Turn the page for a sneak peak at

KEYHOLDERS #2

THE OTHER SIDE OF MAGIC

1

"Can she breathe? Quick! Somebody do CPR!" Buttercup the rat cried, putting her paws on her cheeks in rat panic. She gnawed on Natalie's shoe-laces.

Natalie sat in a kitchen chair in the middle of Mr. Leery's kitchen. Her mouth opened and closed like a guppy, but no sounds came out. A pink notebook slipped from her lap and smacked onto the floor, startling the rat on her sneakers.

Penny and Luke stared at Natalie. They had never gotten along with their neighbor and fifth-grade classmate, mostly because she always bragged about everything her dad bought her. But that didn't mean they liked seeing Natalie gasping for breath.

"Well, this is going well," Mo said sarcastically. Mr. Leery's black cat sat on top of the counter. He lifted a huge paw and casually cleaned the tuft of hair between his ears.

"Hush, Mo," Mr. Leery said. "The girl has suffered a shock. Give her time to get used to the idea. I'm sure she'll be fine."

"Natalie Lawson has never been fine," Luke muttered. "And she's never been speechless, either."

Penny swatted Luke on the arm. "Well, there's a first time for everything," she said. "Now, be nice."

"Why?" Luke asked. "It's Natalie. She's never nice to us."

"Oh dear, oh dear," Mr. Leery said, bending down in front of Natalie and snapping his fingers in front of her eyes. "Talk to me, child."

Natalie's eyes slowly focused on the old man.

For as long as anyone could remember, Mr. Leery had lived in this small cottage at the dead end of the last street in Morgantown. Everyone thought he was harmless. Luke and Penny knew he was much more than that, and now Natalie was beginning to find out how deceiving looks could be.

"Rats," Natalie mumbled as she gradually remembered where she was. "I saw rats. Here. Your house. It's infested. With rats. Must tell. My father."

"No, no, no," Luke said. "Don't you remember a word of what we told you?"

Penny and Luke had helped Mr. Leery explain everything to Natalie. But as soon as she'd seen the dragon and unicorn she'd totally blanked out.

"This isn't a rat," Penny said, pointing to the animal perched on Natalie's shoe.

"Yes it is," Mo purred. "A big, fat, juicy one."

Buttercup squeaked and gnawed on the lace edge of Natalie's sock.

"Shh, Mo," Mr. Leery said. "You're not helping."

Penny started over. "Okay. This *is* a rat. But it's not a normal everyday kind of rat. She's your link. Just like Kirin is my link."

At the sound of her name, a unicorn clomped into the kitchen from the living room to gaze at Natalie. "How many times do we have to go over this?" the unicorn snapped. "I'm hungry."

"And Dracula is my link," Luke added, ignoring Kirin's complaint.

"That's me! That's me!" sang a dragon the size of a Doberman pinscher as he flapped into the kitchen. The kitchen was too small for his wings and he ruffled everyone's hair as he searched for a place to land.

"They came from the other side of the border," Penny explained.

Everyone in Morgantown knew about the thorny bushes at the edge of their town that had been there for as long as they could remember. What they didn't realize was that the bushes formed a magical border between what was real and what was magic. The only people who were allowed to know were the Keyholders, a force of three whose job it was to maintain the border.

"Mr. Leery chose us as the new Keyholders," Luke said. "It's going to be our job to make sure magic stays out of our world."

"But to be a Keyholder you have to be chosen by a link from the other side of magic," Mr. Leery added. "And this very special creature chose you."

Natalie glanced down at Buttercup. The rat stopped gnawing long enough to give Natalie a small wave with her paw. The color faded from Natalie's face and she shuddered. She looked up. Her eyes landed on the unicorn peering over Penny's shoulder.

"Back up," Penny told the unicorn. "Give Natalie some room to breathe."

When Kirin took a step backward, she trampled Dracula's tail. Dracula swooped up, knocking over a pitcher of water from the counter. Buttercup squeaked as the pitcher smashed to the floor within inches of her tail. Kirin automatically tossed her head at the high-pitched sound, her horn catching in the curtains and ripping them off the window.

"Enough!" Mr. Leery bellowed and raised his arms. The room fell silent.

Except for Natalie. Natalie whimpered.

"I would not have placed this burden on you at this time if it wasn't an emergency," Mr. Leery said. "But it is. Two Keyholders are gone and I can no longer protect the border by myself. I need your help, Natalie. Yours and Penny's and Luke's. Unfortunately, we'll have to wait to have your official ceremony. For now I will give you this for . . . protection." Mr. Leery took the bracelet from his wrist. It was silver like Penny and Luke's, but this one had a purple stone. It was a perfect match to the collar dangling from Buttercup's neck, the very one that used to hang on Mo.

"That silver will keep the boggarts and goblins away," Kirin said with a nod of her horn. "That and bells work every time."

Dracula flapped his wings so that he could hop up and down. "Bell! Bells! I like bells!"

"But I don't want to be what you said," Natalie whispered. "A Keyholder."

"Too late," Luke said. "You already are one. The rat picked you."

Buttercup spit out a shoelace. "Just barely in time. I say, *barely* in time," she babbled. "Because the Queen of the Boggarts is out to get us, one and all!"

About the Authors

Marcia Thornton Jones enjoys reading more than anything else. As a teacher, her favorite part of the school day was sharing books with her students. It was that love of reading that drew her to writing. She wanted to write the same kinds of stories that she and her students enjoyed reading. One afternoon she mentioned to the school librarian that she'd always had an interest in writing. The librarian, Debbie Dadey, shared a desire to write stories that would encourage reading skills while promoting a true joy of reading. The next afternoon, Marcia and Debbie met while their students were at lunch and began writing. That story, "Vampires Don't Wear Polka Dots," became the first book in their bestselling series The Adventures of the Bailey School Kids.

Marcia lives in Lexington, Kentucky, with her husband, Stephen, and their two cats. For more information about Marcia, her books, author visits, and for activities related to her books, check out Marcia's Web site: **www.marciatjones.com**

D EBBIE DADEY taught first grade before becoming a librarian. It was while teaching that she first realized how much she wanted to write a book for reluctant readers. Her first book, co-authored with fellow teacher Marcia Thornton Jones, was about a mysterious teacher. Since then, Debbie and Marcia have collaborated on more than 125 books with sales of over forty million copies.

Debbie lives in Bucks County, Pennsylvania, with her husband, Eric, three dogs, and three children. Her Web site is **www.debbiedadey.com.**